Itsy-Bitsy Cloud
A Secret Wish Granted

Francis Edwards

Ukiyoto Publishing

All global publishing rights are held by

Ukiyoto Publishing

Published in 2022

Content Copyright © Francis Edwards

ISBN 9789362698179

All rights reserved.
No part of this publication may be reproduced, transmitted, or stored in a retrieval system, in any form by any means, electronic, mechanical, photocopying, recording or otherwise, without the prior permission of the publisher.

The moral rights of the author have been asserted.

This is a work of fiction. Names, characters, businesses, places, events, locales, and incidents are either the products of the author's imagination or used in a fictitious manner. Any resemblance to actual persons, living or dead, or actual events is purely coincidental.

This book is sold subject to the condition that it shall not by way of trade or otherwise, be lent, resold, hired out or otherwise circulated, without the publisher's prior consent, in any form of binding or cover other than that in which it is published.

www.ukiyoto.com

Dedication & Acknowledgements

Dedicated To The Memory of Lee Barry Turner

Withdrew from this Earth, February 7th, 2022

My now, Guardian Angel. He kept telling me to write everyday during his sickness to keep my mind occupied and away from his troubles. He heard on Earth the good news on February 7th, 2022, ""Congratulations, your book has been accepted for publication"".

Lee Barry Turner will be with me every step I take along my lifetime journey of writing storytelling books, essays, and poems for children, until our souls are bonded together in the Heavens above by the grace of God.

Illustrations searched from Google

Credit given where noted from these searches:

Unsplash photos of Clouds:

Daoudi Aissa
Barrett
Scanner
Oskay
Emmanuel Appiah
Patrick Janser
Vladimir Anikeev
Nicole Geri
Josiah H
Julian Reijnders
Yurity Kovalov

Illustrations also downloaded from source royalty free, commercial use:

The Graphics Fairy

Free Vector Images

Pixels

Pixabay

Peakpx

Created illustrations using:

Text on Image

Clip Art Free Download

Thank you all for opening your doors to writers to use.

CONTENTS

Itsy – Bitsy's Secret	1
Itsy – Bitsy Writes A Poem	10
Itsy – Bitsy's Tells Her Secret	13
The Deep Dream	17
Visit With The Brownies	19
The Apple Tree Fairy Chieftain	23
Leprechauns	28
War Of The Gnomes	33
The Elves	38
Chain Link	44
Kelpie, The Horse	49
The Storm	51
About the Author	52

Itsy – Bitsy's Secret

Once upon a time, there was a little girl, Itsy-Bitsy, who had such a wonderful spirit. She wanted to climb on a cloud. She kept her secret just to herself. Itsy-Bitsy knew her friends and particularly her older brother, Ziggy, would just make fun of her wish.

Itsy-Bitsy loved to look at clouds. Big white puffy ones always got her attention against a royal blue sky when they slowly drifted by her. She noticed these special clouds used to change their shape, before they disappeared into the horizon. No one understood her fascination. Ziggy used to yell at her to look at the ground while walking to school. "Itsy-Bitsy you're going to fall. What are you looking at? I am going to tell mom!" Itsy-Bitsy would just ignore him and stumble to school. "Ziggy Cloud, just leave me alone, she said".

Once at school, Itsy-Bitsy always asked her teacher for an assigned seat beside a window. Itsy-Bitsy told her teacher she suffered from _claus-tro-pho-bia_. Itsy-Bitsy looked up the word in the dictionary which explained the condition as an extreme fear of a confined space.

Itsy-Bitsy heard the word from her Mother, Merry-Weather, one day, when she was explaining to other mothers at the playground why Itsy-Bitsy is always looking up. Itsy-Bitsy knew this label always worked to secure a window seat in all her classes at school. Itsy-Bitsy only wanted to be able to look out the window to check for passing clouds. Itsy-Bitsy wasn't alone. Other classmates also enjoyed looking out the classroom window, but they were not looking for clouds. Once in a while, Itsy-Bitsy's teachers caught her looking out the window. Those teachers gave Itsy-Bitsy a grave look for daydreaming.

Itsy-Bitsy kept a diary. Every day, if she saw a cloud, she would draw its shape and try to identify the form. Itsy-Bitsy would imagine if the cloud resembled a ship, a country, an animal, a star, a tree or a person. This was her game. This kept her amused for hours on end.

Itsy-Bitsy included clouds in all her drawings. Her Father, Storm, noticed them each time Itsy-Bitsy returned home from school and placed a new drawing on the refrigerator door. Her father would remark, "Itsy-Bitsy your cloud is the best element in the whole drawing. How you do it. I'll never understand".

One of the best times in school for Itsy-Betsy was engaging in her Science class. She loved learning about all the cloud formations. Itsy-Bitsy learned that there are four major categories. Those categories are distinguished by how high the clouds are up in the sky. Itsy-Bitsy wrote in her notebook:

The High Clouds are called Cirrus Clouds, or Feathery Clouds.

Cirrus Clouds are so high any water in the clouds is frozen. Seeing these clouds means stormy weather is on its way or a warm front is coming.

Cirrocumulus Clouds are patchy looking clouds. Good weather is approaching.

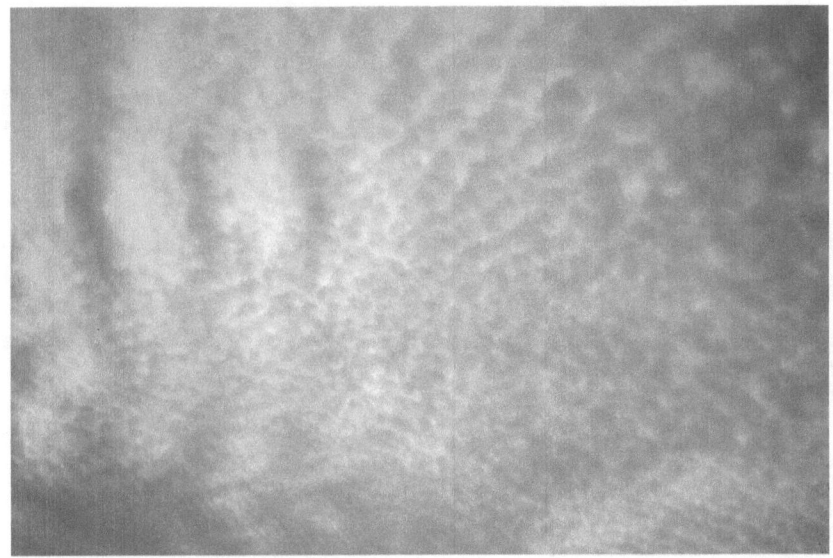

Cirrostratus Clouds are milky looking clouds. The whole sky is covered. You can see through them. This indicates a warm front is on its way. Nice weather.

The Middle Clouds

Altocumulus Clouds are round and oval in appearance. Full of rain. However, the rain just evaporates before hitting the ground. Those Clouds indicate the onset of a thunderstorm. They also mean a cold front is approaching.

Altostratus Clouds are gray blanket clouds. They produce light rain.

Itsy-Bitsy made this picture small, because she doesn't like the look of these clouds at all.

The Low Clouds

Stratus Clouds are fog and mist.

Stratocumulus Clouds are puffy clouds very close together. They forecast
probably a light drizzle.

The Multi Level Clouds display a large vertical up build.

Cumulus Clouds are beautiful clouds that drift along. These Clouds disappear in the evening. They mean good weather.

Cumulonimbus Clouds are vertical mountains.
They forecast storms of heavy rain or hailstones. There even could be a Tornado.

Nimbostratus Clouds block out the sun. These Clouds are very dark. They will produce rain or snow, depending on the season.

Itsy – Bitsy Writes A Poem

Itsy-Bitsy, now can go to her notebook to verify all the different clouds she finds in the sky. Ziggy can't fault her for looking up. Now she can predict the weather. She offers advice to her family, helping them to make decisions, like taking an umbrella. Itsy-Bitsy started making weather predictions into a game. She writes down on her calendar how many times her predictions are correct. Every time Itsy-Bitsy is correct, Storm gives her a coin for her piggy bank. Ziggy has to take out the garbage. Her mother puts an extra treat in her school lunch box. Itsy-Bitsy's cat gives her a special meow, for keeping her safely indoors on predictive rainy days.

Itsy-Bitsy becomes so good at weather predictions everyone at school consults with her, because they can't remember their science lesson on clouds. Mothers at the park, and playground began to consult with her. They would ask Itsy-Bitsy what the expected weather would be. A mother would say, We are in the process of planning outdoor pool parties. Itsy-Bitsy enjoys all this attention. She receives and makes new friends every day. All the newspaper boys, including the mailman ask Itsy-Bitsy what kind of weather are we expecting?

Itsy-Bitsy writes a poem for her English class.

CLOUD, CLOUD, CLOUD...

COME DOWN...

COULD I...

CLIMB ABOARD.

CAN YOU TAKE ME...

CAMPING IN THE SKY...

COME ON DOWN TO ME.

CAN'T BE TOO SOON...

CAN'T WAIT...

CAN KISS YOUR BLESSING...

CAN CELEBRATE YOUR PRESENCE CLOUD, CLOUD, CLOUD...

COME TAKE ME AWAY...

CONTINUE WITH YOUR JOURNEY...

CONDITION BEFORE YOU DISAPPEAR.

Itsy-Bitsy reads her poem to Ziggy, but he is not impressed. He declares, "That poem is crazy, you can't sit on a cloud, you crazy girl, you will fall through it. I am telling mom on you"! Itsy-Bitsy replies, "I can pretend, stupid, now go and take out the garbage before it rains".

Itsy-Bitsy wants to show her father her poem. He is so impressed with the poem, he asks, "Itsy-Bitsy why did you use all those words beginning with the letter C"? Itsy-Bitsy replies, "C is the alphabet letter we are learning at school. All those C words will be on our spelling test next week". "Oh, I see, here is a dollar for your piggy bank. Your poem was cleverly constructed, congratulations. Continue conveying content; claiming copyright".

Itsy – Bitsy's Tells Her Secret

One day, Itsy-Bitsy is asked by her mother to go out in the back garden to pick some flowers for a table setting. Merry-Weather is planning to entertain the local Garden Club at a luncheon this afternoon. While Itsy-Bitsy is busy picking wild flowers, such as blue bells, heather, lupines, and yellow flowers, she can't resist looking up at the clouds. As soon as she does this, Itsy-Bitsy trips over a rusty old garden ornament. She picks it up and sees that it is a Cupid. Cupid is so happy. He was finally found, after spending years and years hidden away. He was rusting away on the damp ground. Itsy-Bitsy placed the Cupid on a large rock. The Cupid said, "You have saved me. For you I will shoot my last arrow. My arrow can pierce the heart of a Garden Fairy, and she may grant you a wish." "Yes, yes, please proceed. I have a secret wish. I have never told anyone, except my cat, Jumping-Jack. He keeps my secret, because he can't speak human language".

Itsy-Bitsy carefully places the rusty Cupid down upon a more comfortable smooth rock, so he could steady himself. The Cupid shot his last arrow directly at a disturbance in a purple flower patch.

"It's a Garden Fairy," declares Itsy-Bitsy. "I can just see her!"

The Garden Fairy flutters above some purple flowers. Now, Itsy-Bitsy can really see her against the royal blue sky. The Garden Fairy always changes her color to match the flower color or thing she hides behind. Today, she is purple. She matches the purple flowers where she hides today. The Garden Fairy tells Itsy-Bitsy, she can only exchange a secret for a secret. The Garden Fairy says to Itsy-Bitsy, "You must tell me your secret first, since my heart is pierced". Itsy-Bitsy says, my secret wish is to climb upon a cloud and drift along in the sky. The Garden Fairy replies, "My secret is that I can't grant wishes, but I can ask for your wish to be granted by your Godmother Fairy. She is the only one who can grant your wish. Since your last name is Cloud, your Godmother's name is Cloud. You will know her. She will come to you dressed in a beautiful white cloud looking gown, carrying a magical wand with a star attached."

The Garden Fairy tells Itsy-Bitsy, "I promise to inform your Godmother Cloud your secret wish, while you are in a deep sleep some night. This is when I'm allowed to speak to your Godmother Cloud, on your behalf. Your Godmother Cloud could enter a deep sleep any time soon and perhaps grant your wish." You must tell no one about this. If you do, then your wish will be gone. Your Godmother Cloud will not enter your sleep no matter how deep your sleep becomes. Your sleep will not have any dreams, if the secret is found out. You must remember this each day and every hour in the day, not to tell anyone.

The Garden Fairy hears footsteps. She must go. She must fly away and hide among a purple color flower patch. She just disappears as quickly and fast as she appeared.

Itsy-Bitsy turns around and sees her brother, Ziggy. He shouts, "Why are you taking so long, mom needs those flowers right away. Hurry up, Itsy-Bitsy or I'm telling mom on you. You can't be depended upon to do anything"!

Itsy-Bitsy gets all flustered. She hurries off with an arm full of flowers. She doesn't even take the time to place them in a wicker basket that she brought with her. Itsy-Bitsy is so happy. She doesn't know what to think. She knows only one thing for sure. She must not tell anyone her secret.

The Deep Dream

Every night Itsy-Bitsy's mom would say to her daughter after reading a story book, "Sweet dreams my dear". No dreams came. Poor Itsy-Bitsy could tell no one about her secret. The only one who knew was her cat, Jumping-Jack. He could only meow. Itsy-Bitsy remembered what the Garden Fairy said, "The secret would disappear like a Cumulus Cloud, if any secret was even slightly echoed even during a snore".

One night, Itsy-Bitsy started to toss and turn in her sleep. Jumping-Jack started to meow and meow, louder and louder. The Godmother Fairy Cloud appeared. "I have come to grant you your secret wish. Now you can rest in peace, my dear child. You have passed the test. You have not told a soul about any secrets of ours or yours. Many children have asked for your secret wish, but they all have failed. You have resisted all temptations. You have proven yourself to me. Those other children couldn't keep that secret wish to climb on a cloud. All their hopeful clouds turned into rain. Their wish was rained out. They can't climb onto their once chosen cloud. Their wish has vanished forever. You are lucky. Your cloud awaits.

The mountain where I live is the capital of Fairy Land. I am the Queen of Fairy Land Mountain. I have instructed my mountain to make you a Cap Cloud. Once you start your climb to the mountain I will, with my magic wand, direct upward winds to the peak of the mountain to form your Cap Cloud. Your cat will let you saddle him. He can then jump on the cloud.

The Clap Cloud will take you to my world, called the Other World. You will visit my Kingdom. To confirm your arrival, in each Other World Terrain, you must give a postcard. Those postcards will contain the addresses of all the fae you will visit. Once visited, the terrain postcard will be flown back to me by the Garden Fairy who told me your secret wish. This will confirm your visit. Clap Cloud will move onward to a new terrain with different fae people, with you and Jumping-Jack on board. If the Garden Fairy comes flying back to me, without a postcard signed by the head chieftain of each terrain, the Cap Cloud will drift on without you and Jumping-Jack. You and your pet cat will forever be living within the terrain fae in my Other World. You will never leave. All my subjects pledge to keep secrets to themselves. No one in your human world will ever find out where you are in my Other World Kingdom.

Godmother Cloud has another rule fairies all must follow. Fairies never lie. Truth must be told.

"Now off you will go!"

Visit With The Brownies

The Clap Cloud drifts across the sky and hovers over farmland. Itsy-Bitsy and Jumping-Jack can see farm animals, a barn, and a farmer's house. Itsy-Bitsy thinks to herself, "How wonderful". She asks Cap Cloud, "Is this the first Terrain"? "Yes, now make sure you take the right postcard marked Brownies with you, when Jumping-Jack takes you off me".

Itsy-Bitsy and Jumping-Jack arrive and are greeted by Brownie Hard Worker, "Welcome"! "It's nice to see an extra helping hand on the Farm Terrain". "Your beautiful Persian Cat can carve himself a home away from home. He can jump into that large pumpkin over there. I think he will quite like to nestle there."

Brownie Hard Worker explains that the farmer, with my help at night, has gathered up all the pumpkins from the fields. You have arrived for the pumpkin carving time. Pumpkins are carved with faces on them. They are lit with candles at night to scare the spirits away. Spirits are not faeries. Spirits could be ghosts, witches, devils, vampires, or zombies that scare animals on the farm. They appear out of nowhere, on October 31st. Humans call the occasion Halloween. Your job will be to carve faces on 50 pumpkins. Each pumpkin must have a different scary face carved. Now, I must go and tell the Farmland Terrain Head Chieftain that you are here. Good luck my dear. See you later. Start carving out pumpkins as soon as you can. Here is a carving knife. Be careful not to cut yourself. Oh, by the way, your cat can deliver each carved pumpkin around to each animal pen. Make sure you provide a few extra pumpkins for the pigs. They always eat a few before Halloween night.

Hard Worker heads off to tell the Farm Terrain Chieftain that the Clap Cloud has brought a visitor from the human world to carve pumpkins.

"There here, there here," yells Hard Worker. Her name is Itsy-Bitsy Cloud. She will carve pumpkins for us. Look, she has already started.

Head Farmland Terrain Chieftain is disguised as a scary pumpkin. When he greets Itsy-Bitsy, he explains to her that his position on Halloween night is to protect the farmer's home from any evil intruders. I must stay on the farmer's porch. Please don't be alarmed about the way I look. After Halloween, I will return to look like a normal Brownie with pointed ears. Itsy-Bitsy is just too frightened to hand him her postcard. Jumping-Jack runs to his pumpkin and jumps inside. Itsy-Bitsy decides to wait until after she carves 50 pumpkins.

Itsy-Bitsy continues to carve and carve pumpkins. She soon starts to run out of different faces to carve. She carved out Ziggy's face ten times! Ten different ways. Itsy-Bitsy tells Jumping-Jack to deliver most of the Ziggy pumpkin faces to the pig pen. Itsy-Bitsy hopes that the pigs are hungry. By the time she reaches 33 faces, poor Itsy-Bitsy starts to cut out different clouds on the pumpkins. She thinks storm clouds may scare off the witches. The witches will be afraid to fly during a storm.

Itsy-Bitsy, after helping the Brownies, wants to <u>cloud on</u>. Itsy-Bitsy finds a clever way to deliver her postcard to the Chieftain. Itsy-Bitsy places her postcard inside one of her carved pumpkins to show the Chieftain her handy work. The Hard Worker delivers the pumpkin to the Chieftain, and as he lifts up the lid to place a candle inside, his hand seizes the postcard. He signed the postcard and the Garden Fairy, who is now orange in color came fluttering out of some stacked pumpkins and took the postcard under her wings. The Garden Fairy disappears from sight to deliver the postcard to Godmother Cloud.

Just a few hours before sunset on Halloween night, the Cap Cloud appeared and Jumping-Jack took Itsy-Bitsy on his back and jumped on the Cap Cloud. Itsy-Bitsy was so happy. She knew any goblin who was ghunting around the Farm Terrain Halloween night would scare Jumping-Jack. Jumping-Jack could run away and hide somewhere on the farm and never be found. Itsy-Bitsy even believed the pigs could eat Jumping-Jack instead of a Ziggy faced pumpkin.

Itsy-Bitsy played a trick on the Chieftain in Halloween tradition. No lie was told. Itsy-Bitsy's treat was the Clap Cloud arriving just before sunset. Itsy-Bitsy and Jumping-Jack could see all the lighted pumpkins around the farm along with a lot of strange shadows as the Clap Cloud moved away during a full moon, star lighted sky.

The Apple Tree Fairy Chieftain

The Cap Cloud doesn't go very far. It starts to hover over a thick forest full of huge old trees. The Cap Cloud stops. Itsy-Bitsy and Jumping-Jack spring off into a dense dark forest. Itsy-Bitsy begins to follow a path she finds between some trees. The trees look like they have been growing there for a hundred years or more. They have huge trunks, like the elephants in a zoo. Itsy-Bitsy begins to notice that some trees have knots on them resembling what look like faces. She also begins to think something is hiding behind some of the trees. Jumping-Jack starts to meow at one particular giant Apple Tree. Jumping-Jack will not move forward at all. The poor cat is just frozen to the ground. He just keeps looking up and meowing a very scary sound. Itsy-Bitsy hears the same sound from Jumping-Jack just before a cat fight. The meow becomes a hissing sound. Jumping-Jack hunches his back getting ready for battle. Itsy-Bitsy is frightened. She, like Jumping-Jack, becomes frozen and starts to shake. She wants to run away, but can't move.

The old Apple Tree begins to talk in a very hollow deep pitched voice. "You have come upon the Dryads Terrain and I am the Chieftain Apple Tree. Don't worry. We Dryads never step outside our trees. We become part of the tree when a knot transforms into a face.

I am the only Dryad with eyes that can see you. My eyes let me see the children from your world who try to hide behind trees out of my sight. I believe some of the children who say they lost their postcards are lying. While others are afraid to give me their postcards, because they are afraid of my looks or voice which is more to the truth. All those children must stay here forever. They are stuck here. They all survive on nuts or the apples that have dropped and rolled away along the ground away from my trunk. They are too used to the sweet words spoken from their mothers. My deep hollow voice keeps them away from my tree. "Are you afraid of me?" "No, but my cat, Jumping-Jack, is afraid. I have a brother who sometimes has a low hollow voice just like yours. His voice especially goes deep when he threatens to tell my mom on me".

The children from behind the trees slowly come out to greet Itsy-Bitsy and Jumping-Jack. Itsy-Bitsy was told by her mother to try and help less fortunate children.

Itsy-Bitsy asks for the postcard from each child . Itsy-Bitsy relates to the children in a whisper. I am going to play a trick on the Tree Chieftain. I promise all of you will be <u>clouding on</u> with me. The children respond, "The Chieftain Tree will use his branches to chase us. We will not make it to your cloud." Itsy-Bitsy replies, "Oh no he won't, he does not lie. The Garden Fairy will receive all your postcards to fly back to Godmother Cloud, if my trick works". Itsy-Bitsy says, "Playing a trick is not fibbing".

Each child hands over their postcard to Itsy-Bitsy. Once this is done. Itsy-Bitsy on Jumping-Jack's back leap up the backside of the Chieftain's Tree. The tree doesn't feel a thing. Itsy-Bitsy, with the help of Jumping-Jack, hides one postcard behind each leaf with tree sap. Itsy-Bitsy chooses leaves that are autumn gold or orange.

Itsy-Bitsy waits until a gentle breeze comes through the forest and shakes the loose leaves from the forest trees. When the Chieftain gets the falling leaves hitting his eyes, he takes a branch to grasp the leaf away from his eyes. Those leaves have a postcard attached. Itsy-Bitsy and Jumping-Jack leap up and down with joy. Itsy-Bitsy exclaims, "Look children, my trick worked!

The Garden Fairy, now dressed in green and autumn gold, comes fluttering down from a branch. She takes all the postcards signed by the Chieftain Dryad. The children all jump up and down with joy. Itsy-Bitsy, "You're so very, very clever. Now we can leave with you and your cat. Thank you, Thank you!"

Itsy-Bitsy and Jumping-Jack are both happy too. Itsy-Bitsy won't have to travel alone, she will have new friends to talk with. Jumping-Jack will have lots of attention with cuddles and hugs.

Soon enough, the Cap Cloud appears and Jumping-Jack carries on his back five new friends to <u>cloud on</u>.

Itsy-Bitsy is so happy to have friends to talk to that she writes a poem to remember the old Apple Tree.

A for Apple, Apple, Apple

Apple Tree...

Able to see red...

Allow to have...

A lot to take.

Away with them...

A good tree...

Account to replace...

Another year will come.

Always a good treat...

Apron on...

Apply good measure...

According to instructions.

Access the...

Aroma to ignite ...

Appetite...

Approval to follow.

Applause...

Allows you another...

Add your blessings for...

Apples, Apples, Apples.

Leprechauns

Across the sky the Cap Cloud went with the Trade Winds, pushing the children all the way Eastward across the Atlantic Ocean from a terrain in North America to Europe. The sleepy children are taken to the home of the Terrain of Leprechauns, that hunams call Ireland.

These shy fairies are entirely made up of all males. They have been a part of the Terrain Leprechaun before any humans appeared living there. The Leprechauns have become a symbol adopted into modern day Ireland. There are many Irish stories written about them in Irish folklore.

The children are slowly awakened by hearing music and dancing that seems to get louder and louder. They hear tapping like hammers keeping time to the music. The children are now all wide awake and want to join the fun. The children are glad to land on solid ground. The children had <u>cloud lag</u>. Time marches backwards when traveling Eastward. They quickly got over feeling tired. They are surrounded by the friendly Leprechauns. This is their way of welcoming newcomers to their terrain. One Leprechaun even held up a sign for all the children to read.

"Children, you are all welcome to refreshments and join our party." While you are busy having fun, we cobblers are going to make you new shoes. We know children wear out their shoes very quickly. This will be our gift to you. We will make the cat a new collar from the scraps of leather shoes. Itsy-Bitsy replies, "How wonderful, thank you so much". Jumping-Jack adds his meow. All the children clap and start to dance around acting silly.

Itsy-Bitsy soon realizes that every time she blinks her eyes, the Leprechaun that she is talking to disappears. Itsy-Bitsy thinks to herself, " How am I going to give six postcards to the Chieftain Terrain Leprechaun, if I blink". I can't stop blinking. I know I must play a clever trick.

Itsy-Bitsy asks a Leprechaun, "What is done to our old worn out shoes"? The Leprechaun replies, "We let the Chieftain Terrain Leprechaun decide. We will give all your old shoes to him and our Chieftain Leprechaun will sort them out, according to condition. If anything can be reused, we will save them from becoming winter fuel. Our little houses in villages all across our Terrain are heated by old unrepairable old shoes".

Itsy-Bitsy puts her legs crossed to think. She knows from reading lots of storybooks that no one has ever caught a Leprechaun and received a pot of gold. In fact, no one in the last thousand years has ever caught a Leprechaun, she remembers reading somewhere or maybe Ziggy told her. Itsy-Bitsy doesn't want a pot of gold. Gold will not let the Cap Cloud come to pick her up with her new friends, anyhow. Itsy-Bitsy must think of a way to pass the postcards into the hand of the Chieftain Leprechaun.

Itsy-Bitsy knows all fairies love gifts. Itsy-Bitsy secretly gathers up all the children's postcards. She places each postcard in the right shoe of each pair. She gives the right shoe from each pair into one box and wraps the box with paper requested from one of the Leprechauns. The gift paper is covered with four leafed green clovers, a good luck symbol used by the Leprechauns. Itsy-Bitsy puts all the left foot shoes in a bag and gives the bag over to a cobbler. She presents the wrapped gift to the Terrain Leprechaun Chieftain. Itsy-Bitsy says without blinking, "Chieftain Terrain Leprechaun, please accept this humble gift from all the children from the Cap Cloud in return for entertaining us and your kind hospitality". The Chieftain shakes the box first then opens to see the shoes. He is delighted by such thoughtfulness. He inspects each shoe and receives the postcards. He happily puts his signature on each one. Itsy-Bitsy sees the Garden Fairy emerge from behind a four leafed clover. The Garden Fairy is dressed in all green and takes the postcards and flies away with them.

Itsy-Bitsy eventually runs to all the children, who are now dancing in their new shoes. She alerts them to the approaching Cap Cloud. Jumping-Jack is purring with his new blue collar with added width for strength. The children will feel more secure holding on to it, whenever they are being transported onto the Clap Cloud.

Itsy-Bitsy writes another poem in honor of this happy occasion.

B for BOOK, BOOK, BOOK

Believe me, I will read...

Best to enjoy...

Better than playing...

Be my friend.

Becomes my aim to read...

Beyond my knowledge...

Behind my past...

Begin a new adventure.

Brighten any hour...

Becken my thoughts...

Broken my...

Boredom.

Brave little...

Book, Book, Book

Bind the pages...

Bond the story for me.

Believe in Leprechauns.

War Of The Gnomes

The Cap Cloud was able to launch into the deep clear pure blue sky. This time, the Cap Cloud asked Itsy-Bitsy, "Where in the Other World would you like next to take your friends?" "Please take us to the Gnome Terrain. I know Gnomes are friendly. They like to have lots of fun. I have Gnomes at home in my back garden. Ziggy always trips over one, while chasing me. He always blames me and says, 'I am going to tell mom on you'. All of us would be happy to visit them. I am sure of it".

Looking over the Cap Cloud, as the Cap was approaching land, Itsy-Bitsy saw a huge sign.

Itsy-Bitsy decided to let the five children on the Cap Cloud take a vote, before landing in this new terrain. This would be the best solution, since the vote could not turn out to be even. The vote was taken by a show of hands. The Green Gnome Hats won.

Itsy-Bitsy was happy with the decision, since a Green Hat Gnome was holding the sign! Upon being delivered by Jumping-Jack, Itsy-Bitsy asked the Gnome what the fighting was all about. The Gnome stated, "The war was started up by humans. They were only purchasing Red Hat Gnomes for their gardens. Many Green Hat Gnomes became jealous. The Green Hats have taken up hammers to smash the Red Hats to eliminate them from store shelves. Humans will only have one choice to buy Green Hats. Green Hat production from our factories have been in decline for some time now and that has caused unemployment and hardship for many Green Hat Gnomes". The Gnome Terrain has two Chieftains, one Red Hat and one Green Hat. The Chieftain who wins the battle will appear here, near the sign and declare victory. Stay hidden until you see a horse approaching. Only the two Chieftains have a horse.

Itsy-Bitsy turns red in the face. Her mother just purchased a Red Hat Gnome for the back garden. Itsy-Bitsy now wants to paint the hat green, after she gets home. Ziggy probably will say, "I am going to tell mom on you"!

Itsy-Bitsy and the five children can't see any battle, but they can hear smashing ceramic hats being knocked off statues in the distant field. The Green Hat Gnome tells all the children. If you are scared, go hide in the holes dug beside the roots of trees in the forest over there. The Red Hats are advancing this way and could break our line of defence soon. You see, our fighters are weaker than the Red Hats. We haven't had any food to make us strong fighters. The situation becomes apparent. The battle front noise gets louder and louder. All the children decide to run and hide in the holes around the roots of the trees near the huge sign. The children remember their punishment for breaking things in their homes. They want no part in a battle between the Red Hats and Green Hats. The children may be punished harshly after getting home.

Out of the now quiet battlefield, a Chieftain Terrain Gnome, on a horse, appeared without a hat just in front of Itsy-Bitsy and Jumping-Jack.

Just before all the children ran to hide, Itsy-Bitsy collected their postcards. Itsy-Bitsy remarked to the Chieftain, "you lost your hat". "No", he said back, laughing. "I took it off to protect me from being smashed by friend or foe". Itsy-Bitsy took an educated guess from all the information that was given her from the Green Hat Gnome. Itsy-Bitsy picked up a red hat she found close by and placed the postcards inside the hat. The Terrain Chieftain put the hat on and received the postcards.

The Terrain Red Hat Chieftain told Itsy-Bitsy that a truce was declared and the battle ended. The Red Hats will engage human stores with an offer to customers that if they buy one Red Hat they will get a Green Hat at half price. This plan will keep the Green Hats happy and their workers busy making Gnomes. Everyone wins.

The Garden Fairy now looking red and green came out of a green hat and flew off with the signed postcards. After all, the children attended a truce celebration. The Cap Cloud came and hovered over the party long enough for all the children to be carried on by Jumping-Jack.

H for Hurdle

Heaping on you...

Headed your way...

Hold on.

Have the resolve...

Head for trials...

Hit the target.

Hope for the best...

Hatch another plan...

Hail that one if successful.

Heap that hurdle down...

Hide it behind...

Having another one to face?

Half the list has gone…

Hop to another discovery…

Here comes another secret.

Happy you will be…

Hard not to resist…

Helping others.

Hats of Red…

Hats of Green…

Have your choice…

Home garden will embrace.

The Elves

The Cap Cloud skimmed across another very blue sky with all the children hanging on. This time the Clap Cloud took a Northerly direction straight towards the North Pole. All the children felt the cold temperature and grabbed extra blankets and jumpers (sweaters) to keep warm. Most of the children had Green Hats from the Gnome Terrain on their heads. One of the children knew who lived in the North Pole and yelled his name, Santa Clause. The children heard him loud and clear. Itsy-Bitsy and Jumping-Jack could see the excitement on all their faces.

The first sighting the children saw after landing were the Reindeer. Yes, all nine of them. They were instructed to take the children to the Terrain Kingdom of Santa Clause. The problem was that they could not deliver on the instruction from Santa. There were more reindeer than children. The reindeer could start a fight over which reindeer would get to select a child. The reindeer snorted and kicked up a fuss. Itsy-Bitsy knew what to do. She had the five children make two snowmen. Now each reindeer had an occupant to transport - 6 children, 2 snowmen, and Jumping-Jack. Now all was well.

Off the reindeer went through the snow to Santa's Kingdom with their cargo. Upon arrival, the children were welcomed by the Elf, called Ify. Ify would say, "Ify you do that, I will do this". Ify never did anything on his own. He always needed help or told everyone first what to do. He said to Itsy-Bitsy and the children, "If you line up, I will open the Santa Kingdom's door. If you hold out your hand I'll get the elves to shake your hand. If you tell the elves your name, I will tell you theirs. If you go and sit at the table, I will have the cooks prepare lunch for you. If the cooks help me bring food to the table, I will serve the food".

Itsy-Bitsy asked Ify, "Is Santa Claus the Chieftain of the Terrain?". Ify said no, but Santa stands in for the Chieftain Elf. Many years ago, our Chieftain Elf left us. The Seelie Court which settles disputes among the Fairies, ruled that the Terrain Chieftain Elf was to be banished from what we now call, Santa Kingdom, North Pole. Itsy-Bitsy asked, "What did he do"? The Chieftain Elf hated Christmas. He refused to celebrate the season. He told a lie and pretended to like Christmas for years. Itsy-Bitsy then asked, "How did the Other World find out"? One Christmas season, the Chieftain Elf ordered the elves to make all the toys with defects. The Chieftain Elf even altered the instruction to drawings, so that the toys would fall apart. Santa delivered those toys around the world. It wasn't until the next year that the Chieftain Elf was found out. Letters from children came to us from all over the world complaining about the toys they received, from Christmas past. The children included in their letters a wish for toys that contained a guarantee against defects. Those letters were collected and sent by express Garden Fairies to the Seelie Court for investigation. The Court interviewed the toy making Elves. The Elves took their blueprints with them. The blueprints were approved by the Terrain Chieftain Elf.

The Seelie Court also established that the Chieftain Elf took good toys and buried them in the snow. This fact came to light when the Santa Kingdom experienced an early thaw. Toys were found by some Elves. The Elves were having a snowball battle. Those Elves saw toys poking up through the snow. Before the snowball battle, reindeer stomping on the ground, as they do, looking for food to nibble on, broke the toys.

The Seelie Court kept to the rule, one can not live a life of lies. The Chieftain Elf broke the Terrain Golden Rule, not to lie. The Godmother Fairy Cloud sent our Chieftain Elf to the South Pole. She sent two special clouds called Nacreous Clouds. The Godmother Fairy also sent a special message delivered by a Garden Fairy to Chieftain Elf that said, "If the toys are not fixed before arrival at the South Pole, the Nacreous clouds will vanish and disappear. You will fall into the ocean and disappear along with the toys nobody wants". We have a copy of the letter in our Santa Museum. No one has heard from the

Chieftain Elf, but a few toys have been found by some monkeys. Those toys were washed up on a beach in Africa, we heard.

Not one elf wanted to go with the Chieftain Elf on his exile to the South Pole. The Chieftain Elf went as far ordering his elves to leave. This caused a revolt. One night, a group of elves waited until the Chieftain fell asleep. Those elves tied the Chieftain Elf up with ribbons, and bows to his bedchamber. When the two Nacreous Clouds arrived, the elves tied extra ribbons from the bed to a special large balloon. It was made in the toy factory for this occasion. When the balloon reached the biggest Nacreous Cloud, an arrow was shot bursting the balloon. The Chieftain Elf fell upside down. He landed right in the middle of the biggest Nacreous Cloud. The elves did the same trick to the broken toys. Ribbons were tied to balloons and attached to the broken toys. Those balloons were shot with arrows, landing the broken toys onto the smaller Nacreous Cloud.

The elves all celebrated the Chieftain's departure and thanked the nine reindeer for finding and digging up the toys buried in the snow. The reindeer were found innocent by the Seelie Court of all wrongdoing. All the elves stayed in Santa Kingdom making toys.

Santa Clause has never been replaced by any new Terrain Chieftain Elf. Every year we celebrate the Chieftain Elf departure. We call this holiday Upcycle Day.

All fairies from around the Other World send discarded toys found in bins to us. The Garden Fairies fly them in by the hundreds. We recondition those toys and send them out again on Christmas Eve with Santa. All the effort our elves do on those discarded toys helps to stop climate change. Tomorrow is Upcycle Day. You will meet Santa Claus. Ifty says one last thing, "Make sure all your friends and Jumping-Jack make out a wish list to give to Santa Claus tomorrow".

Itsy-Bitsy gets all the children and Jumping-Jack to write their Christmas wish list on their postcards. The next day comes, and everyone is at the festival. There are fireworks, huge balloons, bows made from ribbons, and candy canes everywhere in Santa Kingdom. Inside the workshop, Elves are busy receiving box after box from the

Garden Fairies. Itsy-Bitsy spotted one of her toys that she left outside in the garden, back home. Itsy-Bitsy decided that Ziggy must have told her mother. Her mother must have told Ziggy to throw it in the bin, the next time you take out the garbage. The toy was Itsy-Bitsy's favorite doll.

Itsy-Bitsy puts a request on her postcard to Santa to have her doll returned. The doll is Betsy Wetsey. Itsy-Bitsy got it from Santa Claus a few years ago.

The children greet Santa and give him their postcards. The Garden Fairy appears out of a box and receives the postcards from Santa and a cookie to take with her. Santa asks Elf Ifty to find the doll. Ifty says he will be happy to look for the doll if some elves help him slide down the rolling metal scute, first. Santa said, Ho, Ho, Ho! All the children joined Ifty and tumbled down the shute from the second floor to the first. The children were having such a good time, no one wanted the fun to stop. The Santa Elves gave candy canes and homemade chocolate chip cookies to every Elf and child, if they made it to the bottom of the shute. Ifty pulled a doll from one of the boxes and handed the doll to Itsy-Bitsy. "Yes, Yes, this is my doll, my Betsy Wetsy!" "Thank you Santa"! "Thank you, Ifty"!

This was just in time. While looking out the window, one of the Santa Elves saw the Cap Cloud approaching Santa Kingdom. Itsy-Bitsy told Santa and Ifty that soon all the children will be on their way. Jumping-

Jack ate too many cookies, but he still managed to transport all the children up onto the Clap Cloud. Away they went off into a bright blue sky.

Chain Link

The Cap Cloud descended on Santa Kingdom with specific instructions from the Godmother Fairy to drift the children to the Terrain Chieftain Change Link. The Godmother's Golden Rule for all in the Other World was not to lie. "No one should live a lie".

Itsy-Bitsy is a beautiful child with long golden blonde hair. Her violet eyes were unusual. She was small, but popular at school. Her personality beams with confidence, like sharing her knowledge of weather forecasts. She noticed that all her classmates were all taller than her. Itsy-Bitsy started to ask questions. She quizzed her mother about her small size, one day. Her mother replied, "Don't concern yourself about your size. You will start growing taller soon. You will grow taller during your sleeping hours". Itsy-Bitsy refused to look at herself in any mirror in her home, because in her heart knew she wasn't getting any taller. Itsy-Bitsy had a mark drawn on her bedroom door to her height. No new mark was ever added month after month. Even Ziggy started to tease her and called her, "Shrimpy". Storm, told Itsy-Bitsy not growing any taller keeps you cute for lots of cuddles. Itsy-Bitsy was only four times the size of her doll, Betsy Wetsy! Most children got new clothing every year, because they grew out of them. Itsy-Bitsy, on the other hand, never grew out of her clothes. She was made to wear her clothing until they wore out. Itsy-Bitsy never received new shoes. They had to have holes in the souls. Itsy-Bitsy thought this condition wasn't fair. Ziggy continued getting new clothes and shoes all the time. He kept growing taller and taller every year.

The Cap Cloud finally arrived over Terrain Chain Link. The Cap Cloud announced that the only child allowed off the Cloud was Itsy-Bitsy, since she was the only child with a postcard for the Terrain Chieftain Link. The Cap Cloud could not lie. He knew other reasons, but tried to keep them secret, until a child cried, but why? The Cloud responded, "This terrain is very dangerous. The Fairy Links could take you and do a double switch and then another double switch again and again. Switch you back and forth to your human family or back again to the Other World. You see those Change Link Fairies have a history of switching children. One can not trust them. They give away their fairy children to human parents to raise in exchange for human children. Those Change Link Fairies think their children could receive a better education or have more opportunities presented to them like better food. Maybe, they will perhaps grow taller in the end. This situation is very dangerous for you five children, since you all are on your way to the Human World. Stay on the Clap Cloud. You will be safe with me. I will let all of you play your favorite game, guess what I can see".

Itsy-Bitsy was very brave. She hopped on Jumping-Jack and landed on Terrain Change Link. She perhaps could find the truth. Maybe, she would find out her roots. She could come face to face with her existence. What exactly did the Change Link know that she didn't know? Could she ever know the truth? What questions would she ask? Worse than anything, would allowing her off the Cloud just be a plot to keep her? She would not care if she never saw her brother Ziggy again, but would miss her mother and father. Such thoughts came flowing from her, mixed with tears and tumbling. She tried to calm herself down by thinking that no matter what would come from this visit, she still had Jumping-Jack and her favorite doll, Wetsey Betsy.

Itsy-Bitsy heard footsteps coming towards her from the dense forest that closed out most of the sunlight. The trees around here formed a canopy that permitted only rays of light to touch the ground. With each approaching step, Itsy-Bitsy became a bit more nervous. Finally, the footsteps stopped right under a ray of light. A voice proclaimed, "I am the Terrain Chieftain Change Link. I have brought with me an archive book from our Department of Links. Link Runner is holding the book for you to read.

He will help you to look up your name, Itsy-Bitsy Cloud. Maybe your name is not in the book. Come over in the light to see together what is revealed. Itsy-Bitsy hesitates, but curiosity takes her into the light. Link Runner finds her name in the book and points to the name, Itsy-Bitsy Cloud. The Other World Book states that you are in fact a Fairy, belonging to our Change Link Terrain. The Runner Link goes on to say, you were switched to a human family called Cloud. We had your wings clipped and ears modified so no human could guess that you are a fairy. Itsy-Bitsy burst out crying on hearing this news. "What is going to happen to me?" These words could be heard between her sobs. The Chieftain Link tries to calm Itsy-Bitsy down. The Godmother Cloud has arranged this visit in order for you not to live a lie. No fairy in any Other World or person in any Human World should live with a lie. Truth removes any doubts and provides happiness to your being. The Godmother Cloud, concluded from your questions about your size that it was high time for you to know the truth. Your wonderful personality will not change. You will still be loved in your adopted Human World. No one there will ever question where you came from. Itsy-Bitsy says, "I am still confused. Who was I switched with?" The Chieftain Link responds, "You were switched for a little baby human girl." "Can I meet her?" "No, unfortunately, she passed away a few years ago, because she would not listen. She leaped from her tree house to climb on a cloud. She fell tumbling down to the ground. Like you, she had the same secret wish. However, she didn't wait for the Godmother Fairy to grant her wish".

Itsy-Bitsy asks, "What is going to happen to me, my doll, and Jumping-Jack"? The Chieftain Link tells Itsy-Bitsy that the tragic death of the human switch can now never ever take place with the Cloud family. You will be returned to them, provided you abide by the terms made by the Godmother for your travels around on the Clap Cloud. Itsy-Bitsy is greatly relieved.

Now her only problem is to get her postcard into the hands of the Terrain Chieftain Link. Itsy-Bitsy goes up to Runner Link, one last time to see her name in the book. She knows the Chieftain Link must sign the book to record his meeting with Itsy-Bitsy. She saw lots of his signatures on the various pages that the Runner Link was turning.

Itsy-Bitsy places her postcard on her name page in the book. The Chieftain gets the postcard as he signs the book. The Garden Fairy dressed in newspaper print comes flying from the covers of the book, and claims the postcard. Off she goes with the postcard. Not long afterwards, the Cap Cloud appears just above a tree top. Jumping-Jack claws up the tallest tree with Itsy-Bitsy on his back along with her doll. Jumping-Jack then takes a big leap and lands on Cap Cloud. All the children clap. They are so happy to see her! The children made Itsy-Bitsy a halo from the Cap Cloud. Now the children call Itsy-Bitsy the Cap Cloud Angel. Her new name.

Kelpie, The Horse

The Clap Cloud drifted very slowly towards the North. The children were all asleep, so the cloud took its time arriving towards the new destination called the Kelpie Terrain. The children were all awakened from their deep sleep, when they heard a horse sounding out its distinctive sound. One of the children exclaimed, "Look over there". They all saw a horse-like creature standing on the bank of a river. He was as blue as the water.

Once the Clap Cloud hovered near the horse, each child wanted to be first in line to pet the horse. The horse seemed friendly. Jumping-Jack did his job and placed each child near the horse. Everytime, the horse was petted, he threw his head up and down in gratitude. He appeared very friendly.

One child got the idea to ride him. The child got Jumping-Jack to lift him onto its back. Now, all the other children wanted a ride too.

The horse accommodated this wish by stretching its back to make room, but only enough room for five children. Itsy-Bitsy, being an Angle, stood by the river bank alone and watched each child fill a space on the horse's back. One of the children decided to surrender their space to let Itsy-Bitsy take his seat. The child could not dismount. The child was stuck to the back. All the rest of the children tried in turn to dismount. All were stuck. They were glued to the back of the horse. Itsy-Bitsy was horrified.
Itsy-Bitsy rushed over to the horse. Itsy-Bitsy took all the postcards and tried to pry off the children, one at a time. Each postcard stuck to the horse.
The horse took a gallop into the river. Itsy-Bitsy stood shocked by the river bank. The horse disappeared right into the water. Later, Itsy-Bitsy saw one postcard surface upon the water. It was her postcard.

The Garden Fairy appeared from behind a tree on the river bank, dressed in blue, and fetched the postcard. She flew away with it.

The Clap Cloud soon came. Jumping-Jack quickly delivered Itsy-Bitsy with her doll onto the Clap Cloud.

Itsy-Bitsy, with big tears streaming down her face, declared in a scream, "I want to go home. I have no postcards left".

The Storm

Itsy-Bitsy, like a lot of weather forecasters, can make a mistake. She left her window open in her bedroom. A big rainstorm with high winds formed early in the morning. The rain and wind started to blow the window curtains and rattle the shutters in her bedroom. Ziggy was already up. He was getting ready for school, when he heard strange noises coming from Itsy-Bitsy's bedroom. He stormed into the bedroom and slammed the window shut.

This noise woke Itsy-Bitsy up, out of her deep, deep dream. Ziggy said, "I am going to tell mom on you".

About the Author

Francis Edwards

Francis Edwards has accomplished reformatting the Victoria Tunnel Book into a modern day 3D presentation for storytelling and learning books for children. He has to date 15 Titles. You may go to Etsy.com to purchase one of his Tunnel Books.

His essays, poems, and writings can be read on Medium.com. He also has a presence on Smashwords.com.

www.ingramcontent.com/pod-product-compliance
Lightning Source LLC
LaVergne TN
LVHW041552070526
838199LV00046B/1925